DISNEY·PIXAR

Illustrated by Bud Luckey and Dominique Louis

Story adapted by Andrea Posner-Sanchez

 A Golden Book • New York

Copyright © 2006 Disney Enterprises, Inc./Pixar. Disney/Pixar elements © Disney/Pixar; Hudson Hornet is a trademark of DaimlerChrysler; Volkswagen trademarks, design patents and copyrights are used with the approval of the owner, Volkswagen AG; Model T is a registered trademark of Ford Motor Company; Fiat is a trademark of Fiat S.p.A.; Porsche is a trademark of Porsche; Jeep is a registered trademark of DaimlerChrysler; Mercury is a registered trademark of Ford Motor Company. Inspired by the Cadillac Ranch by Ant Farm (Lord, Michels and Marquez) © 1974. All rights reserved. Published in the United States by Golden Books, an imprint of Random House Children's Books, a division of Random House, Inc., New York, and in Canada by Random House of Canada Limited, Toronto, in conjunction with Disney Enterprises, Inc. Golden Books, A Golden Book, A Little Golden Book, the G colophon, and the distinctive gold spine are registered trademarks of Random House, Inc.
Library of Congress Control Number: 2006920645
ISBN-13: 978-0-7364-2416-5
ISBN: 0-7364-2416-4
www.goldenbooks.com
www.randomhouse.com/kids/disney
Printed in the United States of America   10 9 8 7 6

Mater liked to play pranks
on his friends.

Scary pranks were his favorites!

"Oh, buddy," Mater said to McQueen with a chuckle. "You looked like you just seen the Ghost Light!"

"What's that?" McQueen asked.

Sheriff came forward and told the story of the mysterious blue light that haunted Radiator Springs. "It all started on a night like tonight. A young couple were headed down this very stretch of the Mother Road when they spotted an unnatural blue glow . . . and before long, all that was left were two out-of-state license plates!"

"Don't be too scared, buddy. It ain't real," Mater whispered to McQueen.

"It *is* real!" shouted Sheriff. "And the one thing that angers the Ghost Light more than anything else . . . is the sound of clanking metal!"

When Sheriff finished his story, the townsfolk
said good night and quickly drove home.
Mater was left all alone—in the dark.

Gulp!

The scared tow truck drove to his shack in the
junkyard. Mater thought he saw a monster in the
shadows, but it was just a gnarled tree. He was
trembling and shaking so much that his one good
headlight fell off and broke.

Mater gasped as he saw a small glowing light heading toward him.

"OH, NO!

It's the Ghost Light!"

The light flew right up to Mater's face. He opened one eye to peek at it.

"Oh, it's just a lightnin' bug," he said with a nervous laugh. "And anyhow, Sheriff said the Ghost Light is blue."

"The Ghost Light's right behind me!" Mater screamed.

"Now it's in front of me!" he gasped.

Mater raced through the tractor field.

He sped past Willys Butte.

But he couldn't get away from the Ghost Light.
"The Ghost Light's gonna eat me!" he cried.

A very tired Mater finally came to a stop and saw
that the Ghost Light was just a lantern hanging
from his tow cable. "Hey, wait a minute . . ."

"Gotcha!" McQueen said with a smile.

"Shoot," said Mater. "I knowed this was a joke the whole time."

"You see, son, the only thing to be scared of out here is your imagination," Sheriff told him.

"Yup. That and, of course, the *Screamin' Banshee*," added Doc.

"THE SCREAMIN' WHAT?!?"